THE RI
OF
HEROBRINE

AN UNOFFICIAL OVERWORLD
ADVENTURE, BOOK THREE

THE RISE
OF
HEROBRINE

DANICA DAVIDSON

Sky Pony Press
New York

Copyright © 2016 by Danica Davidson

All rights reserved. No part of this book may be reproduced in any manner without the express written consent of the publisher, except in the case of brief excerpts in critical reviews or articles. All inquiries should be addressed to Sky Pony Press, 307 West 36th Street, 11th Floor, New York, NY 10018.

Sky Pony Press books may be purchased in bulk at special discounts for sales promotion, corporate gifts, fund-raising, or educational purposes. Special editions can also be created to specifications. For details, contact the Special Sales Department, Sky Pony Press, 307 West 36th Street, 11th Floor, New York, NY 10018 or info@skyhorsepublishing.com.

Sky Pony® is a registered trademark of Skyhorse Publishing, Inc.®, a Delaware corporation.

Visit our website at www.skyhorsepublishing.com.

Minecraft® is a registered trademark of Notch Development AB.

The Minecraft game is copyright © Mojang AB.

10 9 8 7 6 5 4 3 2

Library of Congress Cataloging-in-Publication Data is available on file.

Cover design by Brian Peterson
Cover artwork by Lordwhitebear

ISBN: 978-1-5107-0802-0
Ebook ISBN: 978-1-5107-0803-7

Printed in Canada

THE RISE
OF
HEROBRINE

CHAPTER 1

I WAS IN DANGER.

I was alone out here in the fields, but I felt someone nearby, watching me. It made the back of my neck prickle and my hand immediately went to draw my sword—and then I realized I was weaponless.

"Where are you?" I called out, though what I really wanted to ask was, "*Who* are you?"

All the trees were missing leaves. In the distance, I could see an ocean with buildings hovering over the sea. Everything was silent, so silent.

I turned around in a circle, straining my eyes. Monsters, also called mobs, were a real threat where I lived in the Overworld, but they could only come out in the dark. Right now it was sunny and there wasn't a cloud in the sky.

So why did I sense a presence? And how did I know it meant to harm me?

I heard a loud sound behind me and I jumped. Then I realized it was just strains of creepy-sounding music. I followed the music to its source. Behind two dark, leafless trees, I found a musical disc sitting in the grass, spinning.

A music disc playing with no jukebox? I thought, confused.

When I reached to pick it up, a deep voice said, "It's too late."

There was some heavy breathing coming from the music disc. It sounded as if someone had been running. I heard footsteps, but there was still no one.

"It's too late, Stevie," the music disc said. "I have already been unleashed, and the Overworld is doomed."

This time I grabbed the music disc for real, shaking it. "Who are you?" I demanded. This couldn't be some pre-recording, because how did it know my name? And why did it say the Overworld was doomed? My best friend Maison and I had just saved the Overworld from a zombie takeover the other week, so everything should have been okay now.

That's when I noticed a sign just a few feet away. How come I hadn't noticed it before? When I stepped up close to the sign, I made out the words: I AM FREE NOW AND YOU CAN'T STOP MY PLANS.

There was a terrible laughter behind me. I knew who it was, then, because no one else could laugh in such an evil way.

"It can't be," I whispered.

I whirled around and there he was. He had eyes with no pupils, so all I saw were glowing orbs of skeleton white, and when he began to approach me, I let out a scream.

CHAPTER 2

"**S**TEVIE," DAD SAID. "WAKE UP."

When my eyes flew open, I didn't think I'd ever been happier in my life to see my bedroom. Ossie, my cat, was sleeping by my feet, and Dad was standing over my bed, looking annoyed.

"Dad," I sputtered, sitting up in bed. "I had *another* Herobrine dream! This time, I was in a field with no one around and there was this musi—"

"Stevie," Dad said again. "Herobrine is just an old ghost story. You know he's not real."

Of course I knew that. When I was a little kid and Dad and I would go to the village, the village kids and I would each take turns trying to come up with the scariest Herobrine story we could. When we'd race on pigs, someone might say, "Last one gets caught by Herobrine!"

There were a million stories about who Herobrine was and what made him a ghost and the sort of evil

3

deeds he might do. The stories were fun, because even though they were scary, we all felt safe knowing there was no Herobrine.

"It just seemed so real," I said. That wasn't the only thing that was bothering me, though. I'd started having dreams about Herobrine shortly after Maison and I had saved the Overworld, and now it had gotten to the point where I was dreaming about Herobrine every single night.

"I need your help today," Dad was saying.

"He said the Overworld is doomed!" I said, unable to stop thinking about my dream.

Dad sighed. I could tell he thought I was being overly dramatic.

"The blacksmith from the village came to visit me while you were still asleep," he said, as if I hadn't spoken. "Lots of weird things are happening in the village. Trees are losing their leaves, and someone has been stealing people's cows and horses. The blacksmith wants me to come help them investigate."

"Dad!" I said. "In my dream, there were trees without leaves and—"

"And," Dad said loudly, so I'd know to let him finish speaking, "I said I would go over this afternoon after Alex gets here."

I had forgotten that Alex was supposed to be visiting.

Alex is my cousin and she is eleven, just like me. We didn't see each other much growing up, and I think that mostly had to do with my dad and Alex's mom, Aunt Alexandra. Aunt Alexandra and Dad were brother and sister, but they couldn't be more different. And, boy, did they like to compete with each other.

Dad is a farmer, miner, and monster slayer. He prided himself in building the most, having the best farm, digging the deepest, and being able to defeat all the mobs with the diamond sword he made when he was only twelve. He was named Steve, and all the people around here called him "The Steve" because of how good he was at everything.

Aunt Alexandra is the mayor a few villages down, and the way my dad is "The Steve," she is "Mayor Alexandra." Even I wanted to call her that. Her village was thriving, they hadn't had a mob attack since she was elected, and she always ran unopposed at elections because the people loved her that much.

They were both pillars in their communities who did very different things. And they were always trying to outdo each other, but there was no way of keeping track of who won. Because how do you compare running a village to fighting off mobs? They're both important.

Sometimes Mayor Alexandra . . . I mean, Aunt Alexandra . . . would visit and bring Alex with her, expecting Alex and me to be best friends because we were cousins and the same age.

But the thing was, I always felt kind of competitive toward Alex, the way my dad and aunt were competitive toward each other. Alex was always so smart and she liked to go exploring and discover things. When I was a little younger and I could barely make wooden swords, she was already great at shooting with the bows and arrows she made. I knew Alex was hands down more impressive than me.

I especially didn't want to see Alex right then, when I was feeling pretty uneasy and scared because of my dream. Alex would go trekking out in the night with her arrows, so she'd think I was a wimp for getting all shaken up over some silly dreams!

"How long is Alex staying again?" I asked. Dad hadn't been very clear on that before.

"However long it takes," Dad replied. "Your aunt Alexandra said that Alex has been acting up and making lots of problems lately, and she hopes Alex coming here will help set her straight."

"Alex is in trouble?" I said in disbelief. I'd never heard anyone complain about Alex before.

"Alexandra thinks you'll be a good influence on Alex," Dad went on. "Your aunt is very impressed by how you saved the Overworld from that mob attack."

Well, this was definitely different. Aunt Alexandra was impressed with me and wanted Alex to be more like me? I wasn't still in dream land, was I?

"I'll need you to entertain Alex today while I'm in the village," Dad said.

As if on cue, there was a knock at the door. Dad went to answer it and I quickly got dressed, putting on a turquoise shirt and purple pants. I could hear Dad and Aunt Alexandra talking, and Aunt Alexandra sounded as if she was in a bad mood. Picking up Ossie, I tiptoed down the stairs.

Dad and Aunt Alexandra were standing in the doorway, with Alex right next to them, a pained look on her face. She had her bow and arrows slung over her shoulders and she was carrying a bulky bag. It must have been the suitcase she packed for her visit.

"I don't get it," Aunt Alexandra said. "Alex never caused any problems, then all of a sudden she's been nothing but a pain in the neck. She won't listen to me, she goes out at night without asking permission or even telling me where she's going. I've had it up to here with her!"

Alex flushed and looked down. I was pretty shocked myself. Aunt Alexandra was a no-nonsense person, but I'd never seen her be outright mean to Alex like this. Now she was talking as if Alex wasn't even there.

I felt Ossie stiffen in my arms as though something had upset her. "What is it?" I asked the cat. Ossie's ears had gone back and she was starting to growl toward Aunt Alexandra.

"Ossie, no!" I said. She'd never growled at family before. Embarrassed, I put the cat down and shooed her out of the room.

"There you are, Stevie." Aunt Alexandra was just now noticing me. "I'm hoping you can set Alex straight. Why don't you remind Alex of what you did recently?"

I looked at Dad, uncomfortable. He nodded. It didn't look like Alex needed to hear what I'd done, but Aunt Alexandra was staring at me with cold, Do-As-I-Say eyes. So I said, "My friend Maison is from another world and I found a portal to it. She and I were going back and forth between the portals, and something in her world called a computer works as her portal. Two cyberbullies named TheVampireDragon555 and DestinyIsChoice123 hacked . . . um, *broke into* . . . Maison's computer and made their own portal."

It was hard to imagine this had happened the other week, because it still felt so fresh. "TheVampireDragon555 used codes to make it night and unleashed zombies. I guess you could think of codes as computer magic. The village by us was turned completely into zombies. But then DestinyIsChoice123 thought it had gone too far and joined up with Maison and me to stop TheVampireDragon555. We were able to turn all the villagers back into humans and DestinyIsChoice123 and TheVampireDragon555 returned to their world."

Aunt Alexandra nodded. "You see, Alex?" she said. "Your cousin Stevie saved the Overworld, but you've just been misbehaving."

"Mom!" Alex said. "That's what I'm trying to tell you! If we don't do something, the Overworld is doomed!"

CHAPTER 3

MY MOUTH WENT REALLY DRY. "WHAT DID you say?" I asked.

"Not this again," Aunt Alexandra said, rolling her eyes. "She's been going on and on about dreams of the Overworld being destroyed . . ."

"It's true!" Alex cried.

"I don't want to hear another word," Aunt Alexandra said. "I have a village to run. You're going to stay here with Uncle Steve and Stevie until you learn the importance of being honest."

"I *am* being honest!" Alex said.

Watching this, I kept thinking back to me trying to tell Dad how scary the dream was and how he wasn't listening. Whatever Alex was trying to say, she was so earnest. I believed her.

Dad cleared his throat. "Stevie," he said. "Why don't you take Alex to the spare bedroom and get her settled? I'm going to talk with Alexandra alone for a bit."

There was never any point trying to argue with Dad. I nodded and gestured for Alex to follow me. When we stepped into the bedroom, I saw that Ossie was lying on the bed and looking content. Before Dad had tamed her, Ossie had been a wild ocelot, though these days, she was just a sweet house cat. Now Ossie got up and rubbed against Alex, purring.

"It's really weird that Ossie was growling at your mom," I said, watching Ossie's purr-fest. "My dad says that Ossie is an excellent judge of character."

"No, it makes perfect sense," Alex said bitterly. "You know how my mom said I've changed lately? That's not true. *She* has. Ever since I went exploring and discovered a music disc, she's been angry and mean. The other people in my village have been acting meaner, too."

"Wait," I said, something clicking in my head. "Music disc?"

"Here." Alex set her bag down on the bed and reached inside. She pulled out a music disc, explaining, "I went exploring in some old ruins by my village. I'd never gone there before because Mom said it was too dangerous, but she said I was old enough now. And ever since I found this music disc, my life has been nothing but trouble."

Then I realized the disc was spinning and starting to play in her hand, even though she didn't have a jukebox!

First there were some strains of eerie music. My whole body tensed. It was the music from my dream!

There was heavy breathing. Gasping. Running footsteps. A voice cried out for help. No, this music disc was a little different from the one in my dream. What was going on?

A harsh, deep voice began to speak. The words didn't rhyme, but the voice made it almost sound like a poem, in some mystical, otherworldly way.

"The doom of the Overworld is upon us.
The great ghost-monster awakens.
You know his name and fear it.
He darts out of your nightmares
and leaves signs before you in daylight,
yet he remains out of reach.
Only five can stand against him.
A builder, a dragon, one finding her destiny.
The daughter of politics
and the son of the diamond sword wielder.
Without them together, all is lost."

The music disc stopped playing.

"It's a prophecy," Alex said softly. "That's all I can figure. Unless something is done, the Overworld will soon be gone."

CHAPTER 4

I HAD CHILLS GOING ALL UP AND DOWN MY BODY. "WE have to tell my dad and Aunt Alexandra!" I exclaimed. As soon as they heard this, they'd realize that Alex wasn't being difficult and that we needed to save the Overworld.

"You mean you can hear it?" Alex said, sounding shocked.

I was so worked up that I grabbed the music disc right out of her hands and went bolting down the stairs. Dad and Aunt Alexandra were sitting together in the den, their voices low and serious. They both turned when they heard me come in.

"Listen to this!" I said, but the disc had already begun to play. The eerie music filled the room, yet Dad and Aunt Alexandra kept looking at me as if I was interrupting them and they were annoyed. They didn't even blink at the heavy breathing or cry for help. And when the harsh-voiced prophecy started, Dad said, "Really, Stevie, we're talking here."

"But it's about the destruction of the Overworld!" I said.

"What are you talking about?" Dad said. "It's an old, broken music disc."

I was confused. "What do you mean, it's broken?"

"It doesn't play," Aunt Alexandra said. "Alex keeps bringing it to me saying it has some prophecy on it."

"It's playing right now." I had to raise my voice over the disc, though Dad and Aunt Alexandra were talking normally.

Alex had come slowly down the stairs and was watching the situation with a resigned look on her face.

"Alex, you're not messing with Stevie's head now, are you?" Aunt Alexandra said. "I can't believe you brought that music disc all the way here with you. What's worse is that you've pulled Stevie into your little game."

Alex grabbed me by the arm and hauled me back up to the guest room and shut the door. She looked at me hard, searching my face.

"So you can really hear it?" she asked.

"Yes!" I said.

Alex exhaled loudly. "Then I'm not crazy! I played it for my mom, for her political cabinet, for everyone I could find in the village who would listen. They only hear silence!"

"Huh? Silence?" I said. The music and noises had been loud and clear as day to me.

She gripped my shoulders. "Don't you get it, Stevie?" she said. "The music disc is a prophecy about the Overworld being destroyed, and it only wants certain people to be able to hear it. That must mean we're part of the prophecy. Think about the wording it used!"

"You think you're the daughter of politics because your mom's the mayor, and I'm the son of the diamond sword wielder?" I asked. I thought of Dad's diamond sword, sitting on the wall. I got another chill.

I looked down at the music disc in my hands. It had gone totally silent. "But . . . but what are we supposed to do with this?" I asked. "It doesn't give us any clues!"

"That's where I'm at a loss, too," Alex admitted. "I kept trying to go back to the ruins to see if I'd find another music disc, but Mom forbade me from going anywhere. When she caught me sneaking out, she blew her top off and said she couldn't deal with me anymore and I was coming to stay with you."

That had to have been hard. I thought back on when Dad had been turned into a zombie. Aunt Alexandra was no zombie, though something was definitely off about her today.

"So," Alex said. "What do we do now?"

"We need to go talk to Maison," I said. "Maybe she'll have some ideas."

CHAPTER 5

MEETING MAISON HAD CHANGED MY ENTIRE life and how I viewed the world. If you'd asked me a few months ago how many worlds existed, I would have said the Overworld, the Nether, and the End. It wasn't until I jumped through a strange portal and fell into Maison's bedroom that I realized the universe was much bigger than I ever thought.

Maison's world was pretty weird. Here in the Overworld, things were blocky, but in Maison's world, things came in all different shapes. They even thought the Overworld was just a place in a video game called *Minecraft* that they liked to play. They had computers and cell phones and all sorts of weird technology, yet if you asked them to build something themselves, most of the people would just stare at you and have no idea what to do. They couldn't even build simple things, like beds or swords.

Maison was eleven, just like Alex and I were, but we all looked pretty different. Alex had very pale skin and red hair, and she was blocky like me. Maison and I both had brown skin and black hair, except she had all different proportions. Her face was shaped like an emerald and on her hands she had something called *fingers* that looked like little squid tentacles. She used her fingers to lift things up or type on her computer.

Besides being my best friend, Maison was also smart and brave, so I thought she was a good person to go to. Together, Maison and I had saved both the Overworld *and* her school from mob attacks. It wasn't all scary stuff, though—Maison and I also had lots of fun, like when we built a tree house together not far from my home.

But when Alex and I went back downstairs to ask our parents if we could visit Maison, we were in for a surprise. Aunt Alexandra had already left, as if it hadn't even occurred to her to say "Goodbye" to her daughter.

Dad, meanwhile, was getting his toolkit together. "I don't want to see the music disc again, Stevie," he said. "Alex is trying to pull a prank with it. Alexandra explained everything to me."

I started to argue that I really did hear stuff on the music disc, only for Alex to shake her head. She knew it was a lost cause.

"We were going to go visit Maison," I said. "Is that okay?"

"What?" Dad said. He was looking for something in one of his chests. "I'm busy, Stevie. I need to go to the village to help the blacksmith with all the mysterious things going on."

"So it is okay?" I asked again.

"Sure, fine, be back by dark," Dad said absent-mindedly. I don't think he was even listening.

On top of everything else that was going on, I was a little nervous about showing Alex the portal to Maison's world. So far, only Dad, Maison and I knew where the portal was located, and we wanted to keep it a secret. I learned that the hard way when a bunch of mobs got through the portal and attacked Maison's school in her world.

"You know you can't tell anyone about this portal," I said to Alex as we hurried toward it.

Alex made a zipping motion over her mouth. "I won't tell anyone, but it's hard to believe you really found a portal to a new world. In my village, there were whispers that you were with some strange-looking humans when you saved the Overworld."

"Well, Maison and Destiny helped me save it," I said.

"Destiny? Like the DestinyIsChoice123 person you mentioned earlier? Is that the same person?"

"Yeah," I said. "DestinyIsChoice123 is her screen name and Destiny is her real name. She and Maison are friends now, but I haven't seen Destiny since then."

"And the other one who attacked the Overworld?" she said, wide-eyed. She adjusted her toolkit and the quiver she had over her shoulder. "TheVampireDragon555?"

I gritted my teeth at his name. TheVampireDragon555 was the screen name of Destiny's cousin, a seventeen-year-old cyberbully who'd masterminded the whole Overworld takeover. After he'd been defeated and returned to his world, Maison said he'd owned up to his mom about all the bullying and griefing he'd done. Griefing was a new word I'd learned, and it meant destroying someone else's stuff for the fun of it. He was seeing a therapist now, and Maison said he was like a new person. Still, I didn't believe that someone as rotten as TheVampireDragon555 could ever really change.

But I didn't get a chance to respond to Alex because something caught my gaze. "Oh, no," I whispered. Just ahead of us was the tree house Maison and I had built . . . and all the leaves on the tree were gone.

I dashed up the ladder, into the tree house, with Alex right behind me. The tree house had been ransacked, the furniture all knocked over and the objects pawed through. Had something been stolen? I frantically began searching through the clutter.

"Oh my goodness," Alex said when she saw the damage. "This is just like what happened at my village. All the leaves are vanishing, and someone's ransacking people's houses."

I looked up sharply. "Your mom didn't mention anything about that."

"She probably told Uncle Steve when we went up to the guest room," Alex said.

Something white was on the balcony. In the bright sunlight, it was almost blinding to read, and as soon as I did, I couldn't turn my eyes away. Alex followed my gaze and inhaled sharply.

There was a white sign on the balcony. In big, scribbled letters it said: I'M GETTING CLOSER.

CHAPTER 6

E VEN MORE PANICKED, ALEX AND I RACED TOWARD the house the portal was in, the sign in my hand and the music disc in hers. Normally when you moved a sign, that made the writing go away. So I was shocked to see those nasty, taunting letters stay right there as if nothing could erase them.

"There it is!" I told Alex as the house came into view. This was the building Dad, Maison, and I had built to keep the portal to Maison's world protected and to stop mobs from going through. I unlocked the house, and together we approached the portal.

"So this is it," Alex said, out of breath. She squatted down and moved her hands over the stone edge of the portal. "What a rare kind of stone!"

"I'm going to see if Maison's home first," I said. "If she is, I'll go all the way through the portal and you follow me. It works like any other portal."

The middle of the portal was glowing red, blue, and green. Portals to the Nether glowed purple and portals to the End looked like a starry night, and this red-blue-green portal was the only kind like it in the Overworld.

Putting my hands to each side of the portal, I stuck my head through the middle. My vision exploded in sky blue, earth green, and then red, the color of spider eyes. The next thing I knew, my head was sticking out the other end of the portal and into Maison's world. And Maison's face was just a few inches from my own.

"Stevie!" Maison cried, jumping back. She put her hand over her heart. "You scared me."

She was sitting at her desk and must have been working on her computer. My head was now sticking out of her computer screen and the rest of my body was still in the Overworld. It must have looked pretty funny.

"Sorry to interrupt," I said. "But something really bad is happening in the Overworld, and my cousin Alex is here with me. We need to see what you think."

Maison took a few steps away from the computer and gestured for us to come in. I pushed myself forward and tumbled onto the carpet of Maison's bedroom. Since her computer was a few feet above the floor, this was always awkward.

"'I'm getting closer'?" Maison read on the sign. "Who wrote that?"

"That's part of what we're trying to figure out," I said. "Things in the Overworld just aren't right! All the leaves are gone in our tree house and someone went through the place and left this sign."

But Maison was distracted by movement from the computer. Alex was pushing her way out of the computer screen, tumbling to the floor as clumsily as I had.

"Maison, this is my cousin Alex," I said, reaching down and giving Alex a hand. "Alex, this is Maison."

Maison had been shocked the first time I'd fallen through her computer and she'd learned the *Minecraft* world was real. These days, she was pretty used to unusual things. Alex, on the other hand, was overcome by the newness of this world. She gave Maison a quick "Hello" and gaped at her surroundings.

"This is . . . extraordinary!" Alex said. She seemed to forget all the danger we were in. Instead, she started poking around the room, looking out the window, touching the walls.

"I would love to go exploring here," Alex said. "There must be so much to find." Then she paused and held up the music disc, becoming serious again.

"We're hoping you can help us, Maison," Alex said. "I know you and Stevie have saved both our worlds in the past. Look."

"I've never seen a real one of these," Maison said, taking the music disc. "Just ones while playing the game. Do you have a jukebox we can play it on?"

That's when the music disc began to play, and Maison went silent. I watched her face. Her eyebrows creased when she heard the first creepy notes, and when it got to the prophecy, she was spellbound.

"I've opened some music discs with creepy music in the game," Maison said. "But this beats all. I've never heard anything like this."

"That's because there *isn't* anything like it," Alex said. "It's a prophecy, I'm sure of it! And you can hear what's playing!"

"Alex and I have been the only ones who can hear it so far," I told Maison. "We tried sharing it with our parents, and all they hear is silence."

Maison turned the music disc over in her hands, studying it. "Let me try something," she said finally. "Stay here!"

She dashed out of her room and down the stairs. "Mom!" she called. "Mom!"

Maison's mom still hadn't met me and didn't know about the portal. It was all too hard to explain. Downstairs I heard her reply, "Yes, Maison?"

"Listen to this." The music started playing. Maison's mom said over it, "That looks like a toy from that game you like to play. *Minecraft,* right?"

"Shh, can you hear it?" Maison asked.

"Hear what?" her mom said blankly.

"The heavy breathing and the footsteps!"

"I have no idea what you're talking about," her mom said. "I don't hear a thing. Did one of the kids at school give that to you? Do you have the receipt? You should return it to the store for not working."

Feet dragging, Maison came back upstairs. "My mom couldn't hear a thing, either," she said. "Do just kids hear it, maybe?"

"No," Alex said. "I shared it with some of the other kids in my village, and they couldn't hear it, either."

Alex and I quickly filled Maison in on the other details.

"It almost sounds like someone's griefing," Maison said. "That would explain the leaves and people's houses being messed with. But that wouldn't explain why villagers are being mean."

Maison got on her computer and began Googling things. "Let me see what I can find."

Alex stared at the computer. "What kind of sorcery is this?" she asked. "Your portal also gives you information?"

"It's a computer," I said. "Hers just happens to be a portal, too. A computer is like a . . . a . . ." I tried to think of a comparison. "I guess it's like a big magic book, because you can get all sorts of information on it. But you can also use it to harm others, like griefing or bullying people through it."

I could tell Alex was still having a hard time following this. I didn't blame her—it took me forever to understand computers, too!

"I can find stuff on music discs in *Minecraft*," Maison murmured, biting her lip. "But nothing like the one you have. Let me try searching the key words 'griefing' and 'leaves.'"

She tried a few more Google searches. Then some images popped up on the screen and I pulled back. There he was. Those white eyes! That awful stare!

"Herobrine!" I cried.

CHAPTER 7

"HEROBRINE?" MAISON REPEATED. "YOU MEAN you have Herobrine in the Overworld?"

"He's just an old ghost story," Alex said. "When I was little, older kids used to scare me with stories and say that Herobrine would get me in the night."

"Do you have Herobrine in your *Minecraft* game?" I asked Maison, feeling the panic of the dream rising up in me.

"No," Maison said. "He's just a hoax. I don't know how he got started, but he's not really in *Minecraft*. People just say he is and come up with all sorts of creepy stories about him. Like he's a ghost or he's a virus."

"He's a sickness?" Alex said.

"No, a computer virus," Maison said. "It's something that can damage your computer and keep it from working right."

"If he's not really in your *Minecraft* game," I said, "how come there are pictures of him in it?"

"Oh, these?" Maison said, looking back at the images on her computer screen. "You can just put a mod of him in there. That means you 'modify' the game. People put images of him in the game and try to trick people into believing he's real."

"What can you find out about Herobrine?" I asked Maison.

Her fingers flew over the keys of her computer. She opened up some webpages and skimmed them. "Not a whole lot," she said. "He's like an urban legend. There's no canon on him because he's not real. So one person will say this is true about him, and another person will say something totally different is true about him."

I was feeling sweaty. I wiped my head.

"Are you okay, Stevie?" Maison asked, concerned. "You look really sick."

"Yeah," I said, but my tone sounded more like I was saying the opposite. "It's dumb. I've just been having dreams about him . . ."

I trailed off. I expected both Maison and Alex to be like Dad and tell me to get over dreams about some made-up ghost. However, both of them cringed and then looked at me with wide, telling eyes.

"I've been having dreams about him, too," Alex said. "Ever since I found the music disc."

"This last week," Maison said, "I've had a nightmare about Herobrine every night."

I couldn't believe I was hearing this. No wonder the dreams had gotten under my skin so much . . . if Alex and Maison were dreaming the same thing, these were more than regular dreams!

"What happens in your dreams?" I gasped.

"I'm by myself and I feel really scared," Maison said. "Then Herobrine pops out at the last minute."

"Same," Alex said.

"Does he talk to you?" I asked.

They both shook their heads.

"He's talked to me in my dreams," I said. "At least, I think it was him talking. He said that the Overworld is doomed and there's nothing we can do about it. The dreams must be the connection to this prophecy. It makes sense now."

"This still doesn't make sense to me," Alex disagreed. "How could a make-believe ghost be behind all this?"

"That's not the only thing," Maison said. "How do you defeat something that's hurting you but isn't even real?"

CHAPTER 8

MAISON REACHED FOR HER PHONE. "I'M CALL-ing Destiny," she said. "She knows more about computers than I do, so maybe she can help us figure this out."

A moment later Maison said into the phone, "Destiny, this is Maison. Uh-huh. Look, Stevie and his cousin Alex are here . . . Yes, that Stevie. He's here from the Overworld. We need to talk with you right away. Can you come over here?" Pause. "Ask your mom or dad if they can bring you over. Okay, I'll wait."

Alex was staring bug-eyed at the phone.

"Is she ill?" Alex asked me, her voice low enough so Maison wouldn't hear. "She's talking to herself."

"No, she's talking to Destiny," I said. "It's a phone. It lets her talk to people who aren't nearby."

"Wow!" Alex said, impressed. "I wish we had stuff like that in the Overworld. It would make life a lot easier."

"Okay, see you soon," Maison said, and hung up the phone.

Fifteen minutes later, Destiny's dad dropped her off. Maison led her up to the bedroom, where Alex and I were waiting.

Destiny was wearing black like the last time I'd seen her, but her whole personality was different. She seemed a lot happier now, and she even hugged me when she saw me. There was still something about her that was kind of shy, though. It was like she didn't always trust herself to speak up, even when she knew she had something important to say.

After brief introductions, we filled Destiny in on what was going on.

"Can you hear this?" Alex asked, playing the music disc. The now-familiar music began to play, and each time I heard it, it felt worse. It felt more real.

"Yeah," Destiny said. "There's heavy breathing and stuff."

Then she got silent for the rest of the music disc.

"Oh, no," she said, tugging at her necklace uncomfortably.

"And we've all been having dreams about Herobrine, which makes it even weirder," Maison said.

"You've been having dreams about Herobrine?" Destiny squawked.

"You mean . . . ?" I couldn't finish the sentence. I already knew what was coming next.

"I've been having nightmares about him for a week!" Destiny said.

"I wondered if you knew more about Herobrine," Maison said.

"What's there to know?" Destiny said. "He's a hoax someone made up years ago that caught on online. There are stories that Herobrine will ruin your crops. There are even stories that he'll kill you! He always wants destruction. He's like the ultimate griefer."

"So he's kind of like your cousin, TheVampire-Dragon555," I said. I couldn't help getting in a jab at him.

"No," Destiny said. "Herobrine is much worse. And my cousin is doing a lot better these days, since he started seeing a therapist. Didn't Maison tell you?"

I grunted. That was my way of saying Maison had told me, but I didn't believe it.

"Let me see what I can find," Destiny said. She got on the computer, her fingers flying. She was an even faster typist than Maison, but everything she was Googling was bringing up the same old information Maison had found.

"Maybe it's just a coincidence that we've all been dreaming about Herobrine," Destiny said. "You know, we've all been under a lot of stress because of the attack on the Overworld."

"Except I wasn't involved in that," Alex said.

"Hmm." Destiny bit at her fingernails. "I hate to say it, but we have to talk to a real expert on computers and gaming."

"You don't mean . . . !" I began.

"Yes," Destiny said, wheeling around. "We need to talk to my cousin, Yancy."

CHAPTER 9

"**Y**ANCY?" ALEX WHISPERED TO ME.

"TheVampireDragon555," I said through gritted teeth.

"The feared being who broke into the Overworld, turned it to night and almost destroyed it is named *Yancy*?" Alex said.

"He's been interested in Herobrine for years," Destiny said. "He knows a lot about him."

"Maybe they're working together," I shot in.

Destiny shook her head. "Yancy hasn't been back to the Overworld. He knows he's forbidden from returning and he respects that."

Respect? Don't make me laugh. Whether you called him TheVampireDragon555, Yancy, or "the feared being," it was all talking about the same guy, and he was trouble.

"Let me call him," Destiny said, and Maison handed her the phone. Alex watched curiously, still trying to understand how phones worked. Destiny hung up and sighed, "No answer. We should go over there."

"Just show me the way," Alex said, adjusting her bow and arrows over her shoulder.

Maison and Destiny exchanged uncomfortable looks.

"What?" Alex demanded.

"We can't just go walking out in daylight with you and Stevie," Maison said. "People will . . . stare. And they'll want explanations. It's hard enough trying to cover for the fact I brought Stevie to school with me earlier this year."

"We could cover them in blankets, like ghosts," Destiny said. "It's almost Halloween, so people might think we're celebrating early. I don't think that would be too weird."

"I've had enough talk," Alex said. "Let's go."

But Destiny stopped her.

"What now?" Alex demanded. "This is an emergency. We need to understand what this music disc is telling us."

"Um, you can't walk down the street with bows and arrows," Destiny said.

She might as well have told Alex to stop being a redhead. "What?" Alex said. "How do you defend yourself against mobs if you do not carry weapons?"

"There aren't any mobs in this world," I said.

"No mobs!" Alex said. Her mind was blown.

Maison pulled some white sheets out from her closet. "Here," she said to Destiny. "You make ghost outfits for them. I'll go ask my mom if it's okay for us to walk over to a friend's. Then we'll have to slip out so she doesn't see Stevie and Alex with us."

"You're going to make us ghosts with a sheet?" Alex said skeptically. "Where is your crafting table to do such things?"

Destiny looked pained. "You're not really going to be ghosts. They're just costumes for Halloween. See, look out the window at all the houses on the block. They all have jack-o-lanterns on their porches."

Alex and I peered out the window. Sure enough, most of the houses had little orange jack-o-lanterns out front, just like the kind Dad would make by putting a torch and pumpkin on the crafting table.

"Ah," Alex said. "You have pumpkin farmers here."

"What's Halloween?" I asked.

"Just put on your costumes," Destiny said.

It turned out TheVampireDragon555 only lived a few streets away from Maison. That didn't mean getting there was easy. It was so hard to see through those sheets! Maison held my hand and Destiny held Alex's. They had to guide us.

"Stop here," Destiny said when we'd gotten to a street corner.

"Why?" Alex said. "Do you not understand we need to hurry?"

Right then, a bus flew by on the street, going so fast it made the bottoms of our sheets ruffle up.

"A mob!" Alex said. She reached for her bow and arrows, almost knocking off the rest of the sheet. "I knew it!"

"No!" Destiny said, pulling the sheet back down. "It's a bus. That means it's like a big car."

"A big *what*?" Alex said.

"A big Minecart," Maison said.

"Your Minecarts are noisy in this world," Alex said. "And what is that awful smell it leaves behind?"

"Look, the light's green," Maison said. "Let's go."

"What light?" Alex asked. "Do you have lights that shoot up to the sky and show people where you are?"

"Shh!" Maison said. "People are already starting to stare."

Maison and Destiny led us a couple more streets before stopping in front of a doorway. I pulled the sheet up enough so that I could see, making sure the sheet still covered my back so no one from the street would be able to make out who I was. Destiny rapped her knuckles on the door and we waited.

Alex pulled her sheet up over her head, too. "This is where the feared being lives?" she breathed. "I was expecting something a little more . . . sinister."

She had a point. TheVampireDragon555's house looked like any other house on the street. It even had a jack-o-lantern out front, and the jack-o-lantern's face had been turned into a toothy smile.

When the door opened, I thought of TheVampireDragon555 the night he took over the

Overworld. His skin had been a ghoulish zombie green and his eyes were a deep, dark red. He'd held a diamond sword in his hand as he led the whole zombie army. I cringed.

But standing here was just Yancy, your average seventeen-year-old for this world. His skin was its normal color, his eyes were dark brown instead of red, and he was wearing black jeans and a sweatshirt, no shoes or socks.

When he saw me, he smiled. "Well, well, well, Stevie," he said. "I never thought I'd have the honor of seeing you again."

I wanted to tell him to wipe that smirk off his face. That's when Destiny said, "Be real, Yancy. Stevie and his cousin Alex traveled all the way from the Overworld because someone is threatening to destroy their world."

"Hey, it's not me," he said. "I haven't even played *Minecraft* since then. All I'm doing today is studying for the pre-calc test I'm taking tomorrow and I was getting ready to make myself a snack."

I glared at him. "I don't know why we should believe you, TheVampireDragon555."

"Please, it's just 'Yancy' now," he said. "I gave up my old lifestyle."

"You are the feared being?" Alex asked, blinking. "I expected someone more fierce-looking. But you do look like the pictures."

"The pictures?" Yancy repeated, not understanding.

"Your image is in every village in the Overworld," Alex said.

"Like a Wanted sign," Maison said. "So if you ever step foot in the Overworld again, they'll be looking for you."

"Well, nice to know I live in infamy," Yancy said. "But pre-calc won't study itself . . ."

He started to close the door on us.

"Wait!" Destiny said, putting her foot in the doorway. "We need to ask you about Herobrine."

Yancy groaned, but he opened the door to let us in. "My parents are going to be back soon, so you can't stay too long," he said. "I'm supposed to be studying. My mom's been really down my throat about raising my grade in math."

He lankily made his way into the kitchen and we all followed him. Alex and I took our sheets off and draped them over the backs of a chair at the dining table.

"So, Herobrine, huh?" Yancy said. We all waited with nervous butterflies to see what he had to say. But then something made a "beep" and Yancey pulled his phone out of his pocket and swiped the screen with his finger.

"Hold on, I got to respond to this," he said, tapping at the phone fast with his thumbs.

"Yancy, this is important," Maison said, exasperated. "You can text later."

Yancy kept playing with his phone as if he couldn't hear her or he didn't care. He wasn't taking this seriously at all!

Annoyed, Destiny took the phone out of his hand.

"Hey!" Yancy protested.

"Finish texting when you're done," Destiny said. "We need to talk about Herobrine."

Yancy groaned but didn't try to take the phone back. Agitated, he walked farther into the kitchen.

"What's this sudden obsession with Herobrine?" he said, pulling some jars out of the cabinet. He grabbed a loaf of bread—in Maison's world, the bread came in packaging you bought from the store with green stuff called money. You didn't make your own bread, like Dad and I did.

"Herobrine is this creepy icon from *Minecraft*, but he's not actually in the game," Yancy told us. "He looks kind of like Stevie, only he's bigger like an adult, and his eyes are spooky-looking."

"Who created him?" Destiny asked. She put his cell phone in her pocket. It looked as if she did it without thinking, because she was so interested in hearing what he had to say.

"Beats me," Yancy said. "He doesn't actually do anything. You make up what you want him to do. Some people probably wanted to scare someone else, so they made up this *Minecraft* character and told other people he'll grief you and destroy your stuff."

Just then, Yancy reached into a drawer and pulled out a long, silvery knife that flashed in the light.

I knew he couldn't be trusted! "Alex, your arrows!" I yelled.

Fast as a flash, Alex had whipped out her bow, strung an arrow and held it back so that it trembled, aiming right at Yancy. Yancy put both his hands up, the knife still clutched in one.

"Whoa!" he said. "I'm just trying to make a PB and J with a butter knife. I'm not going to attack you with this."

Alex slowly lowered her arrow. "You better be telling the truth," she said. "I'm a perfect shot."

Muttering under his breath, Yancy unscrewed the lids of the jars and stuck his knife in one, pulling out some gooey purple-red stuff. He spread it on one of the pieces of bread. "I swear," he muttered. "Can't make myself a sandwich without . . ."

"Look, enough about you," Destiny said. "Can you hear this?"

She pulled out the music disc and it played. Yancy stopped making his sandwich to watch her with bored eyes. He must not have heard it, because he had no reaction, just like Dad and Aunt Alexandra.

When the music disc stopped, he turned back to his sandwich. "Nice trick," he said. "Did you buy that at the dollar store?"

"No, it's from the Overworld!" I said. *Does that mean he can hear it?* I thought, my heart pounding. *Of all the people in all the worlds, how come only the five of us could hear this thing?*

"Well, whoever made it has a dark sense of humor," he said, screwing the lids on his jars and dropping his dirty knife into the sink. He took a big bite out of his sandwich.

"Look, I don't think this is a joke," Alex said. "I found it while exploring some ruins. No one else has been able to hear it except for the five of us. The people in my village have started acting really weird, like, really mean. And someone's been breaking into people's houses and going through their things, and the leaves are disappearing from trees. Someone left a sign at Stevie's tree house saying they're 'getting closer,' and Stevie, Maison, Destiny and I keep having nightmares about Herobrine—"

She broke off as Yancy began choking uncontrollably on his sandwich. He thumped himself in the chest a few times, leaning over, an expression of panic on his face. When he managed to swallow the food down, he looked at us all in horror.

"Oh, no," he said, his face gone very pale.

CHAPTER 10

YANCY DROPPED HIS ONE-BITE-OUT SANDWICH on the counter and ran past all of us. When we followed him, he'd gone into what looked like his bedroom and was frantically trying to find something on his computer. His fingers were flashing over the keyboard faster than I'd ever seen.

"Oh, no," he kept saying. "Oh, no, no, no."

"What is it?" Destiny demanded, her voice shrill with worry. If the always-cool Yancy was in a panic, this had to be really bad.

Yancy pulled something up on his computer, read it, and then pounded his fist on his desk. "This is worse than I thought," he said. "Give me that music disc."

Shaken, Destiny did, and we all listened as the disc played again. I didn't think Yancy's face could get any paler, but by the time the disc was done playing, his cheeks were almost as white as the sheets Alex and I had worn.

"We have to go back to the Overworld," Yancy said.

"'We'?" Alex said skeptically. "You're not allowed back."

"What's going on?" Destiny asked. "What aren't you telling us?"

Yancy looked at us wildly. "Herobrine is the ultimate bully, the ultimate griefer, and the ultimate mob. And I think I was the one who unleashed him in the Overworld."

Before any of us could even react, Alex ripped her bow and arrow back out, pointing it at him. "Monster!" she yelled. "You *are* working with him!"

"No!" Yancy said, waving his hands. "I didn't mean to unleash Herobrine. I mean, I did, but not like this!"

"Explain yourself," Alex ordered, her arrow still poised on him.

Yancy swallowed as if trying to swallow down his panic. "When I hacked into Maison's computer and made a portal, I also created a mod of Herobrine and put him in the Overworld. I wanted to see what he would do, but then he just disappeared. I thought it hadn't worked and I forgot all about him."

"How could you *forget* about Herobrine!" Alex said. "Or were you too busy unleashing zombies on the Overworld?"

He swallowed even harder. Right then, I thought he was more scared of Alex and her arrows than he was of Herobrine. "Yeah, uh, um, I guess you could say that," he said. "After Destiny and I left the Overworld, I started having nightmares about Herobrine. . ."

I wanted to grab him by his sweatshirt and shake him. "What sort of nightmares?" I cried.

"He kept showing up and taunting me," Yancy replied. "He said that the new me was just an act, and no matter how much I wanted to change or tried to change, I'd always be cruel on the inside. He said that when I'd created him, I'd created him out of a cyber-bully's anger. I thought it was just a dream and didn't mean anything . . ."

"I've heard enough!" Alex roared, but Maison grabbed the bow before Alex could let her arrow fly.

"Hold on!" Maison said. "What's done is done, and we have to think about what to do to stop Herobrine. Don't you get it? The prophecy is about us."

"The prophecy is about Stevie and me," Alex said. "The daughter of politics and the son of the diamond sword wielder."

"What about the rest?" Maison said. "Remember how it mentions a builder? The word 'mason' means builder. Destiny is the part about destiny. And the dragon . . ."

We all looked at Yancy.

"I have to make things right," Yancy said. "I created him, so I need to stop him."

I was shaking my head. "Oh, no," I said. "I don't believe you. If Herobrine really is doing this, you just want to go back to the Overworld so you can work with him."

Maison looked at me in surprise. "Stevie?" she said.

"I don't trust him!" I said.

"I swear to you, Stevie, I'm on your side," Yancy said, looking at me earnestly.

"He's not the same person you knew," Maison said. "I've watched him change."

"No one changes that much," I said. "I think Herobrine is right: he's still cruel on the inside, and this whole nice-guy thing is an act."

"People can change," Yancy insisted. "But it only happens when they want to change. I didn't change before because it was just a bunch of people telling me how to act, and that made me angry. 'Yancy, do this. Yancy, do that.' But when I was in the Overworld, I saw how I was hurting people. It became real to me then and I promised to stop it."

"I think you only stopped it because you knew you'd lost," I said. "I don't think you honestly wanted to change."

Maison, Yancy and I could have gone on and on arguing. To tell the truth, I felt offended and betrayed that Maison was taking his side at all, even after he admitted releasing Herobrine was his fault. My first thought was always to trust Maison, but this was crazy!

Seeing we weren't getting anywhere, Alex cut in. "Okay, here's what I know," she said. "We've all been having Herobrine nightmares and as far as we can tell, we're the only people who can hear the music disc. Plus, the prophecy does sound like it's talking about all of us. I think we need to take Yancy into the Overworld with us— "

"No!" I interrupted.

"—and see what we find," Alex continued. "If we need him, we need him, and there aren't other options. And if he tries any funny business at all . . ." She drew back her arrow again for emphasis. ". . . then he's mine to deal with."

Yancy looked as if he couldn't tell what was more dangerous: Alex's sharp arrows or the fierce expression on her face. We might not have known whether we could trust him, but Yancy obviously knew he could trust Alex to keep her word.

"All right," he said. "Keep your arrows out if it makes you feel better. I don't want to go to the Overworld, I don't want to fight Herobrine, and I don't want to have arrows shot at me. I'd rather stay here and study pre-calc, which shows you how much I just want to be left alone. But I'll go into the Overworld where I'm not wanted, I'll fight a mob I'm terrified of, and I'll risk the arrows because I know I need to do something to stop Herobrine. Didn't you say before, Stevie, after I attacked the Overworld, that it's always important to do the right thing?"

CHAPTER 11

I COULDN'T BELIEVE I'D BEEN OUTVOTED. TWENTY MIN-
utes later, we'd returned to Maison's bedroom, and
Alex and I took off the sheets we'd been wearing on
the walk back. Yancy had packed a backpack with "sup-
plies" that included his computer ("Just in case the Overworld has WiFi," he said) and some more sandwiches
he'd made ("In case we get hungry while we work," he
said).

When we got to Maison's house, Maison, Destiny
and Alex also decided to put the music disc in his backpack because it was easier to carry it that way. This
really set my teeth on edge.

"That's our clue on how to defeat Herobrine!" I
protested as Maison slipped the music disc into the
backpack. "Don't let him have it!"

"It's less likely to break this way," Maison said.
"And if anything attacks us, we need to have both
hands ready."

"So this is where the magic happens," Yancy said, eyeing Maison's computer.

"Less talking and more going," Alex said, poking him. "We don't have much time."

I went through the computer portal first, followed by Maison and Destiny. Yancy came out second-to-last, and then Alex came through.

"Let's go!" Alex said. She took off running, and we all hurried behind her.

When we got close to the house, I noticed a sign sitting propped against the door. My heart went into my throat. In the same writing as the last sign, it said, I GOT HER, STEVIE. SHE'S MINE NOW.

She? As the others were reading the sign, I tried to think of who "she" was. Maison, Alex, and Destiny were all with me, safe and sound. Dad and I were the only people who lived here, so obviously it wasn't a sign about him.

Then it hit me. "Ossie!" I said.

I sped up, throwing the door open. I had to be wrong. No, Herobrine wouldn't have stolen my cat the way he'd been stealing other people's cows and horses.

But then I thought, *Of course he'd steal Ossie. He knows how much she means to me, and he's the ultimate griefer.*

I called Ossie's name. She had to still be here. She had to be! I'd call her name and she'd come walking over, purring, because she was just fine, Herobrine hadn't gotten to her, I was just letting my imagination run away . . .

Suddenly, Dad appeared in the doorway, hulking over me.

"Stevie!" he yelled. "Where have you been? I told you to stay here with Alex!"

I was so startled by what he said that it took my thoughts away from Ossie for a second. "No, you didn't," I said. "I said Alex and I were going to visit Maison and you said it was okay as long as we were back before dark."

"Don't lie to me!" Dad said. "If I'd said something like that, I would remember! I told you to stay right here while I went to the village, and you disobeyed me."

I couldn't remember Dad ever being this mad at me in his whole life. It almost seemed like his eyes were zombie-red. His angry eyes looked at everyone standing behind me, and then they zeroed in on Yancy.

"You!" Dad growled. He unsheathed his diamond sword and thrust it out toward Yancy. "You are not allowed in the Overworld!"

Yancy, sword at his front and arrow at his back, put his hands up in surrender. "I know," he sighed. "Except this time I'm here to help. You see, Herobrine—"

That was the exact wrong answer. Dad blew his stack. "Herobrine!" he hollered. "I've had it up to here with you kids lying to me! Saying that music disc makes noise, talking about that old ghost story Herobrine as if he's real, telling me you had my permission to go when you didn't have any such thing. So tell me this: what did you do with the cat?"

"Ossie's missing?" I yelped.

"She's been gone since I got back from the village," Dad said. "Now, one of you tell me where she is!"

My first thought was to run through the house and look. Maybe she was hiding in a cabinet or under the bed and Dad had somehow missed her. Then I thought, *Dad doesn't miss anything.*

Well, except for all the clues around him that said Herobrine really was a threat.

I yanked up the sign. "Look, Dad! This must be about Ossie! There was another sign just like this at my tree house earlier."

"Don't wave a blank sign at me," Dad said crossly.

"Blank?" I looked at Maison, Destiny, Alex, and Yancy. I could tell from their faces they could all read the sign, and they were as shocked as I was that Dad didn't see any writing there.

"Don't you see, Dad?" I said. "It's proof that Herobrine is real! He's messing with us. He's showing us all these prophesies, but he's not letting you see or hear them so you'll think we're making it up. But we wouldn't make up stuff like this! You know us."

"I know *him*," Dad said, his eyes not leaving Yancy. "And I see you're all friends with him now. What is this world coming to?"

"This world is coming to destruction if you don't listen to us!" Maison said.

"I bet you're the ones behind everything going wrong in the village," Dad said. "All the cattle going missing—hmm, it's you, isn't it? The whole team of you?"

He sheathed his sword, but he wasn't finished. "Get in the house," he said. "All of you. Now."

He had lowered his voice so he wasn't shouting anymore, but it didn't make any of us feel better. The low growl in his tone told us we'd better listen, or else.

The five of us scrambled into the house.

"I'm going back to the village to look for the cat," Dad said. "And I'm getting Alexandra and other people from the village to figure out how to deal with all of you. You five better be here when I return." With that, he stormed out and slammed the door behind himself.

"He's just like my mom," Alex whispered after a moment of silence. "I never lied to her, either, though I couldn't convince her I was telling the truth."

"It's Herobrine, all right," Yancy said, looking dazed. "He's putting everyone in a bad mood and making them suspicious of one another."

"Then why hasn't that happened to us?" Destiny asked. "We're still getting along. Well, mostly." She gazed sideways at me. I figured she must have been referring to the fact I still didn't like or trust Yancy.

"Oh, I think it will happen to us, too," Yancy said. "Herobrine's power is very strong. We have to hold on to our wits and stay true to one another. If we don't, he wins."

"I have to look for Ossie!" I said, and rushed through the house. Maybe the others thought my reaction to Ossie's disappearance was weird, but she was a part of the family. I knew that the Overworld was falling apart, I knew that we had to go confront

Herobrine, I knew that it was all up to us . . . but please, let my cat be okay!

I tore up the house, opening every cupboard and looking under all the furniture. I called out her name, but there was no sign of her. Herobrine had taken my cat, and he'd taken my dad, too, because he'd completely turned Dad against us. Dad was supposed to be my best ally, not someone who thought I was a liar and that I would grief the village. I would never do those things, and the real Dad would know that.

After I'd torn through the house, I slumped on the ground. I was aware of the others all talking amongst themselves, trying to figure out what the best next step would be. Maison came up and put a comforting hand on my shoulder.

"We're going to find Ossie, and get your dad back to his old self," Maison said. "And we're going to stop Herobrine."

I was overwhelmed. "How?" I asked. "We don't even know where Herobrine is. We don't even know how to defeat him if we find him."

Yancy nodded. "There is no canon I know of on how to defeat Herobrine," he said. "We're going to have to find out together."

"I think the first thing we should do is go to the ruins where I found the music disc," Alex said. "There might be more clues there."

CHAPTER 12

BEFORE GOING TO THE RUINS, WE ALL NEEDED to be armed in case anything attacked us. I grabbed the stone swords that Maison and I had made before. Going over to Dad's crafting table, I used two pieces of stone and a stick and made another stone sword for Destiny.

"Um, do I get a weapon?" Yancy asked.

I kept working at the crafting table, finishing up Destiny's sword, and didn't say a word.

"Helloooo," Yancy called over my shoulder. "Earth to Stevie: can you read me?"

"If mobs attack you, just hit them with your backpack," I said bitterly. "I don't trust you with a real weapon. Weapons are only supposed to be used for self-defense if there's no other way to defend yourself. You'd probably use them like toys."

"Ouch, Stevie," Yancy said. "Maybe Herobrine's already getting to you."

I glared at him. No, I was just being careful and realistic. "Come on, let's go," I said.

Alex led us toward the ruins, since she was the only one who knew where they were. As we walked closer and closer, we found more and more trees without leaves. By the time we stood over the ruins, sunset wasn't far off. None of the trees in the area had any leaves at all.

"All right," Alex said in a take-charge voice. "Everyone spread out in the ruins and look."

Yancy started to walk in on his own, and Alex grabbed him by the arm. "Oh, no," she said. "You're looking with me."

Even though we were supposed to spread out, I found myself automatically hanging close to Maison. A few feet away from each other, we dug through debris and pulled up stones.

"I found a map," Alex said from the other side of the ruins. I looked up to see her squinting at a map. "Hmm," she said. "This map is of a place that isn't too far from here. I wonder if there's a connection . . ."

"Let me see that," Yancy said. "It might just be an ordinary map."

"No," Alex said, pulling the map back when he tried to take it. "I've lived here my whole life. I know the landscape better than you."

I found an old chest and opened it, but it was empty. Overhead, the sun was barely over the horizon.

"We have to hurry," I called out, so everyone could hear it. "We're going to have to head back soon."

Maison looked at me in surprise.

"What?" I said. "It's going to get dark soon, and we can't stay out after dark. That's when the mobs come out."

"Stevie," Maison said slowly, shaking her head, "I don't think we have a choice here."

The others were still digging, and I realized what she was trying to say. My first thought had been to run back home for the night and continue our mission in the morning. I was never out at night if I could help it. Home was safe with its iron doors and protecting torches.

But none of the clues would tell us how long we had before Herobrine took everything over. For all we knew, it could be tomorrow.

And if I went back home, I'd have to face Dad . . .

I began scrambling more quickly through the ruins. Even if we were going to stay out during the night tonight, that still didn't change the fact it was about to get a whole lot harder to see. Then we'd really be struggling to search through the ruins. And on top of everything else, we'd have to be watching for mobs.

I heard the crunch of footsteps and jumped up. Maison looked up, too, and she gasped at what she saw. "We're surrounded!" she said.

Even though I felt sick doing so, I put my hands up in surrender because I didn't know what else to do. Mobs hadn't found us, Aunt Alexandra's personal guard had. A group of the finest trained men and women in the area circled the ruins, trapping us in, their arrows all drawn.

"Stop!" Alex said, jumping forward. "Put your arrows down! It's me, Alex!"

None of the armored guards lowered their arrows an inch. Their eyes were cold. They didn't look like the eyes of people you could reason with.

"No one is allowed at these ruins, by order of Mayor Alexandra," one guard declared.

"Mayor Alexandra ordered that anyone who disobeys this order must be dealt with properly," another guard said, her mouth curling into a sneer. "Seeing that you are the daughter of the mayor, we will escort you home where the mayor can deal with you."

I looked desperately at Alex. What were we going to do? It was clear all these guards knew who Alex was, but her powerful connection wasn't helping us at all.

"Look," one guard said, gesturing toward Maison. "That girl is not from this world. Is she the one who stopped the zombie attack at the nearby village?"

The guards all studied Maison thoroughly.

"If she is, she's up to no good now," the same guard mumbled at Maison with disapproval.

Another guard took a closer look at Yancy. "Look, it is the feared being!" the guard cried.

At once, all the guards rushed toward Yancy. He didn't even have a chance to run before they knocked him down.

"I'm here to help!"Yancy sputtered into the ground. "Let me go!"

"You are the feared being," a guard told him. "You are not allowed to ever set foot in the Overworld. Is this not you?"

The guard in front of Yancy pulled a sheet of paper out of his pouch. The paper showed a picture of Yancy on it and the words, ARREST ON SIGHT.

"Well . . . I mean . . ." Yancy said. "I mean . . . that is me, but this is really extreme circumstances. I came here because Herobrine has been unleashed—"

He didn't get a chance to finish.

"Herobrine?" one of the guards scoffed, and they all laughed a How-Annoying-And-Ridiculous-Can-This-Kid-Be? laugh.

"Let him go!" Alex said, storming over. "I am the daughter of the mayor, and I say you have to release him. We're on a very important mission."

Not liking this, the guard with the paper turned his angry face toward Alex. "You may be the daughter of the mayor, but you are not the mayor. You have no power. You're out here before nightfall, against the rules of the village, and you are harboring the most dangerous being ever known to walk the Overworld!"

"Herobrine is the most dangerous being, and we're going to stop him!" Alex said.

"It's a crime to help fugitives wanted by the law," the guard told her. To the other guards, he called, "I'll deal with these four. Take the feared being to the dungeon!"

CHAPTER 13

YANCY WAS DRAGGED OFF TO THE DUNGEON and Alex, Maison, Destiny and I were escorted to Alex's house. As we walked, I kept hearing the guard's words repeating in my head: *You have no power.*

He said it to Alex, but he meant all of us. Alex had tried her best and had gotten us nowhere. I hadn't even tried anything—I'd just frozen up and put my arms up in surrender. And for what? Now Yancy was caged in the dungeon with the music disc and the rest of us were trapped under the gaze of the guard.

I looked over at the others. Destiny looked scared. Maison looked as if she was trying to come up with what to do and couldn't think of anything good. And Alex just looked plain mad. I didn't know for sure what look I had on my face, but I had a feeling I looked pretty hopeless and helpless.

And I couldn't help but notice all the trees we passed were missing leaves. Their branches stretched out eerily to the sky like the arms of skeletons.

The guard stopped us in front of Alex's house. "Go inside," he said. "Mayor Alexandra is working late because a thief keeps stealing people's property. I will go let her know you're here."

"It's not a thief!" Alex said defiantly. "It's Herobrine."

"Herobrine? What are you, four years old?" the guard replied.

He sent us into the house and slammed the door behind us, locking it.

"Quick!" Alex whispered, opening a chest and digging through it for something. "As soon as he's gone, we're out of here! We have to break Yancy out of the dungeon."

"Break him out of the dungeon? How?" Maison asked.

"I've been to the dungeon before," Alex said. She saw Destiny looking at her funny, and quickly explained, "Not as a prisoner! My mom's the mayor, so I've seen a lot of this town."

"Won't there be guards?" I asked.

"Of course there will be guards," Alex said, adjusting the arrows on her shoulder. "Maison and Destiny, I want you to distract them. Stevie, you and I are going to free Yancy."

"Wait," Destiny said, looking frightened. "How do we distract them?"

"They're not used to seeing people like you and Maison so they will be afraid. They may also recognize you and try to lock you up," Alex said. "So if they see you again, they'll chase you. Meantime, Stevie and I will take care of Yancy."

"We will?" I said. I wasn't thrilled that I had been signed up for this job. I had no idea how to break someone out of a dungeon!

"What if we get caught?" Destiny asked.

"Don't get caught," Alex said simply.

Destiny gulped.

"This . . . doesn't seem like the tightest plan," Maison said. I think she was trying not to hurt Alex's feelings. We all thought Alex's plan was crazy.

"Do you have any better ideas?" Alex asked.

We all thought about it. But no one could think of anything better.

"It's hard to come up with a plan when the rest of us don't know the area," Maison said.

"Exactly," Alex said. "Look, there are a lot of bushes by the dungeon. Run in there and get the guards lost. It's getting dark, so they're going to be jumpy and afraid of running into mobs."

"Wait a second." Destiny dug into her pants pocket and pulled out Yancy's cell phone. "I got so caught up in what was going on I forgot to return it to him!"

"I don't think you can make calls to your world from here," I said, not seeing how the phone could be helpful at all.

"No, that's not it. Listen!" She was clicking some buttons on the phone.

Somewhere nearby a zombie hissed. I yanked out my stone sword, looking for it. Had the sun gone all the way down already?

"Stevie, relax!" Destiny said. She was smiling. "It's the phone!"

She held up the phone to me. She had the game *Minecraft* on it, set to night. It was making zombie hisses and moans.

"So if the guards hear that, they'll think they're real!" Maison said, understanding. "They'll run from mobs who aren't actually there!'

Alex looked proud. "Now we're talking," she said.

"There's still another problem," I said. "The guard locked us in here. How are we even going to get out to make it to the dungeon?"

Grinning widely, Alex held up a key. "Oh, just leave that to me."

Minutes later, Maison, Alex, Destiny, and I slipped out of the house, going as quietly as we could. Night had blanketed the Overworld, and above us, a square moon lit our path.

The dungeon was at the edge of the village, surrounded by glowing torches. Built with stone, the dungeon rose only a little ways above the ground, with small, barred windows. Most of the building, I knew, was underground. And that's where Yancy was, trapped.

We hid behind some leafless trees, watching as about a dozen guards marched around the dungeon. In the torchlight, their eyes looked even colder and angrier than they had before. My stomach was fluttering with nerves.

"Stevie, you come with me," Alex said. I half-heard her talking to Maison and Destiny, telling them where we would all meet up when we were done.

Destiny still looked a little nervous, and I think I did, too. Alex and Maison looked determined.

"Follow me and get the phone ready," Maison whispered to Destiny, and the two of them crept to the bushes to our left, drawing closer to the dungeon.

For all the planning Alex had done, there was still one pretty big hole: she still hadn't told me what *I* was supposed to do!

"Alex, what do I—?" I began.

"Shh," she whispered before I could finish my sentence. "Follow me and watch my back. If anyone comes close, let me know."

So I was the watch. I didn't want a big job, then, but I was kind of hurt that Alex had given me the easiest job of all. Did she think I couldn't handle this?

I thought back to earlier, when the guards surrounded us at the ruins and I hadn't done anything. I flushed. *No wonder Alex doesn't think I can handle it,* I thought, humiliated.

In the bushes nearby, zombies began to moan.

It instantly caught the guards' attention. As soon as the guards ran over to investigate, Alex said, "Now!"

We ran for the dungeon and ducked down beside it, near a barred window. Alex crawled to the window and peered inside. "I see him!"

In the background I could hear more zombie hisses and guards yelling, "Where are the zombies? I can't find them!"

Please, just don't find Maison and Destiny! I thought.

"Yancy! Yan-cee!" Alex was trying to call and whisper at the same time so that Yancy could hear her and the guards couldn't. I crawled closer and peeked inside.

The dungeon was dark, dank and scattered with all kinds of old, broken items as if people had been dumping their trash there. Something about it felt even more abandoned and scary than the ruins had. In the middle of the room was a small cage. Yancy was crouched down inside it, hugging himself with his long arms.

Yancy looked up when he heard his name called. "Alex?" he whispered, as if he couldn't quite believe it.

"We're getting you out," Alex said.

She pulled something out of her pocket. Another key!

"I got it from the house," she said. "My mom keeps a few spare keys around."

While I watched, Alex pulled a long lead out of her toolkit. Leads were used to tie animals and lead them around, but I realized she was using this as a rope. Quickly she tied the key to a piece of the lead and tied the lead to one of her arrows. She crouched back down in front of the window.

This was going to be tricky angling, because the window wasn't very big. I looked around, but so far we were by ourselves. The guards were still yelling to one another about how they heard zombies yet couldn't find them.

Finally, Alex got herself angled right and she let the arrow loose. It flew through the window and into the dungeon, embedding itself in the ground inches from the cage. Yancy reached his hand through the cage's bars and grabbed the key.

"Thanks, Alex!" he said. "Even though you've spent most of this evening threatening me with your arrows, you're all right by me!"

"Quickly!" I whispered, even though Yancy couldn't hear me. This wasn't a time to be joking around.

"Now use the lead to climb out of the window!" Alex directed him.

Out of the cage, Yancy grabbed hold of the lead. He started pulling himself out, planting his feet on the wall. When his hands seized the window-sill, Alex and I took his arms and helped pull him out. The windows were made so no person from the Overworld could get through, which meant it was lucky Yancy didn't have a square, fuller body. His different body shape allowed him to just barely slip between the bars.

"Phew," Yancy said.

"Don't think this means I'm going easy on you," Alex said, jabbing him in the chest. "You just have the music disc."

Instead of looking hurt or angry about this, Yancy smiled wolfishly. "Oh, I've got more than that now. Look what I found while in the dungeon."

My heart pounded. He couldn't mean . . . !

Yancy reached around to his backpack and pulled out a music disc. A *new* music disc.

I was about to ask him if it also had a prophecy, but then someone nearby let out a horrific scream.

CHAPTER 14

MAISON AND DESTINY MUST HAVE GOTTEN caught! Alex and I ran in the direction of the screams, not even checking to see if Yancy would follow us.

Around the corner of the dungeon, we stopped in our tracks and crouched down so we wouldn't be seen. One of the guards was pulling Destiny out of the bushes. Destiny still had the cell phone in her right hand, and it continued to make zombie hisses.

"It's you again!" the guard said. "And you duped us with this—this—" The guard didn't know what to call the cell phone, and it made him look even angrier.

Maison popped out of the bushes nearby. "Destiny, throw it to me!" she called as the other guards advanced.

Since the guard was holding Destiny by her left arm, she was still able to throw the cell phone. Maison caught it.

"Stop right there!" Maison called to the guards. "This is magic!"

Alex and I exchanged confused looks. What was Maison doing? Should we go running to help them, or would that get us all caught? If we all got caught, there would be no one to break us out of the dungeon!

The guards looked at Maison warily. They didn't want to believe her, but since they didn't know what the cell phone was, they couldn't really argue.

"You hear how it's hissing?" Maison demanded. "Well, I can make real mobs pop out of this. Mobs you don't even know about."

The guard holding Destiny scoffed this. "You can't make anything come out of that little thing!" he said.

But all the guards jumped back and flinched when the cell phone let out a loud, annoying noise. I recognized it as the sound of a car horn from Maison's world. You could make all sorts of sounds with that phone!

Maison was pressing other buttons, making more sounds. At first the guards were scared, and then they started to get a little wiser. Maison was creating all sorts of strange sounds for sure, but nothing was actually harming them. And no mob was appearing.

"Quit stalling!" a guard said. "We know you're just trying to fake us with that!"

"Uh, sir," another guard stuttered, pointing. "W-what is that?"

Out of nowhere, a tall, dark creature came running toward the guards, waving its long arms and making a terrible roaring sound. It was tall like an Endermen, taller than the guards, and its head was a scowling, angry-faced jack-o-lantern. As it ran, it curled its fingers into claw shapes.

Fingers? Fingers! It was Yancy with a Jack o' Lantern on his head!

The guards, thinking this was the mob Maison had been threatening, let out enormous screams. As a group, they all turned and ran away as fast as they could.

Yancy ripped the Jack o' Lantern off of his head. "Let's go!" he called, and together we dashed off into the night. When we'd run far from the village, we all stopped, panting and exhausted.

"I hate to admit it," Alex said, eyeing Yancy, "but you were pretty brave out there."

"I really had to think on my feet," Yancy said. "I could hear Maison stalling them, and when I saw a Jack o' Lantern nearby, I got my idea."

He looked at Alex as if he was starting to like her, in spite of himself. "It was really nice of you to come back and rescue me," he said.

"Oh, don't get mushy on me," Alex said, not amused. "Of course we had to save you—you had the music disc!" I think she was also starting to respect Yancy, though, especially after he'd come out and saved us.

"Music *discs*," Yancy corrected. "It doesn't mean much to me, but maybe it does to you."

We all leaned forward, wanting to hear. The new music disc began to spin in Yancy's hands and a deep, harsh voice called out to us from it.

"The rise of Herobrine approaches.
He desires the destruction of the two worlds.
Together the five must stand.
Find him you will, if you
follow the map.
The path to the old temple awaits."

Alex let out an excited gasp and yanked out the map she'd found earlier. "This is a clue!" she exclaimed. "This map leads to an old temple past the nearby forests and on top of a mountain. That must be where Herobrine is!"

"So do you know how to get us there?" Maison asked.

"Yes," Alex said with conviction. "I've never gone up there all the way myself, but I've studied enough maps of the area. And there is an old temple on top."

We all looked in the direction of the mountain and the temple. Right then, all we could see was the darkness of night, like some bad omen.

"So now what?" Yancy asked.

"We rest till morning," Alex said. "There's an old, abandoned house I know of not far from here, and we'll sleep there."

Pocketing the map, Alex started off in that direction with strong, purposeful strides.

"Are you sure?" I asked, following her quickly.

"Yes, I like to visit this house," Alex said. "It's not far from some open mines where I like to explore."

"No," I said. "I mean, are you sure we can take a break?"

"I don't think we have much choice," Alex said. "I'm awake now because of the escape, but we're all going to be tired soon. And if we're too tired, we won't be able to fight. Besides, it's too dangerous to walk now. We're lucky we haven't been attacked by mobs yet."

Alex was right that the house wasn't far from where we were. There was still some furniture in it, like a crafting table and a few beds. Inside, Alex declared, "One of us should stay up and keep guard, just to be safe. We don't want any funny business. The rest of you sleep and I'll take the first shift. Then it can be Stevie, Maison, and Destiny. Sound good?"

"You don't want me to guard?" Yancy said. "That's cold, Alex. I thought we were getting along now. I even got you the clue we all need!"

Ignoring him, Alex said, "All of you should sleep now. We have a big day ahead of us."

I couldn't sleep. Instead, I lay there in the dark and listened as Destiny, Maison, and Yancy's breathing all steadied. Yancy even snored a little.

Meanwhile, my mind was going crazy. We'd gotten another clue, but was that enough? What were we going to do when we actually confronted Herobrine?

In the distance, zombies were moaning. Thank goodness for the safety of this house. As I lay there, my mind spinning, I could see Alex's outline as she stood in front of the window, watching the dark sky and landscape.

Slowly, I got up and joined her.

"Oh, Stevie," she said, surprised. "It's not your turn to take watch yet."

"I know," I said. In the moonlight, I could make out her face a little better. "I can't sleep."

Alex looked sympathetic. "I wouldn't be able to, either," she said. "That's why I asked to watch first." She glanced back at where the others were sleeping. "They're not from this world. They still think of Herobrine as a game. I don't think they know what we're all getting into."

"We don't know, either," I said.

"Yeah, true," she sighed.

We stood there and silently looked at the night.

"Stevie," she said. "I'm so sorry about what happened to your dad and your cat."

I put my head down. Thoughts about Dad and Ossie was part of the reason I couldn't get to sleep. "It's not your fault."

"But I mean it. They're all you have, just like all I have is my mom."

That got me thinking about how critical Aunt Alexandra had been of Alex lately. I knew Alex was also hurting, too, though she wanted to put on a brave face and not say it.

"I'm also sorry your mom has been acting strange," I said.

Alex sighed again. "At first, it just seemed like her usual complaints. You know, nothing I ever do is good enough for her. And she doesn't want me to be an explorer, even though that's what I want to be when I grow up."

I was surprised Aunt Alexandra felt this way. "But you'd be a great explorer," I said. "You already are. Why wouldn't she want you to be one?"

"Because she wants me to be mayor, too," Alex said. "It's like I'm disappointing her because I don't want to go into that field. She even seems to think that because I don't want to be in politics, that means I don't take her career seriously or something. I do! She's a great mayor. But she was meant to be a mayor and I'm meant to be an explorer, and I think everyone is good at different things."

Now I was beyond surprised . . . I was shocked! Alex had always seemed way more mature and talented than me, so I couldn't believe that anyone would make her feel like she wasn't good enough.

"I know how you feel," I said. "My dad always said that I was going to grow up to be a farmer and miner like him, and he'd get mad at me when I wouldn't be good at the things he's good at. Lately he's started to realize that maybe it's because I'm not meant to be a farmer and miner."

"Really?" Alex said. "Maybe then my mom will understand someday how much I want to be an explorer."

I could tell I'd taken a lot of weight off her shoulders. The two of us stood there, watching the night, and even though we didn't say anything, it was the closest I'd ever felt to my cousin.

CHAPTER 15

WHEN I STEPPED OUTSIDE OF THE HOUSE, I thought I would be safe because it was daylight. I was wrong.

The first thing I noticed was a sign sitting on the porch that said HERE I AM. And there he was, standing under a leafless tree, stroking Ossie in his arms.

Herobrine.

I felt the anger flood through me like lava in the Nether.

"Give me back Ossie!" I shouted.

I lunged at him with my stone sword. He didn't even try to back away. My sword hit his armor and splintered into pieces. That made Herobrine roar with laughter.

"You think I'm so easily defeated?" he said in a mocking tone. "I'm not. I can keep coming back."

Ossie was twisting her head in one direction, as if she was trying to communicate with me. I couldn't understand what she was trying to say.

"We're going to stop you, Herobrine!" I declared, attempting not to show him my fear. I couldn't believe how easily he'd broken my sword, the only weapon I had on me! I needed to shout to the others to come help, but somehow I couldn't find my voice to do it.

"You believe those silly prophecies?" Herobrine said. "You haven't found all the prophecies, you know, and you won't like what they all say. So don't count your victories yet."

"What do you want, Herobrine?" I demanded.

"Me?" Herobrine said with relish. "At first, nothing. I was created by TheVampireDragon555, and he put me into the Overworld as a mod. I had no thoughts. I watched. I listened. I realized who created me, and why he created me. A cyberbully wanted me to mess up their world. I began to feed on that anger he had. When he asked for help and said he wanted to change, some of that anger started to go away. However, it's always easy to find anger in the world if you want to seek it out. I grew on anger. Everyone gets angry sometimes, but I use that anger to bring out more anger, and to turn people against each other."

"Why?" I demanded.

"Because it's fun," Herobrine said. "Because I can watch people attack each other and it makes me laugh. But this is only the beginning. First, I'm turning everyone against one another. I'm stealing. I'm hurting. Then I'm going to take over the Overworld. It will belong to me and no one else. And it's not just the

Overworld I have my sights on. You're the boy who has the portal. I'm going to use that portal to enter the world of your friends, Maison, Destiny, and Yancy. When I'm through, there will be nothing left."

With a wicked laugh, he disappeared.

My eyes flew open. Another Herobrine dream, and this one had seemed so real! I sat up and saw that Maison, Alex, and Yancy were all asleep. Yancy was snoring a little. The sun was just rising, and Destiny was on-guard, though it looked as if she could nod off at any second.

"Oh, Stevie," she said when she saw me. She yawned. "How did you sleep?"

"Barely," I said. Instead of feeling tired, I felt a strange restlessness. I think it was because of the dream. I kept thinking of the direction Ossie seemed to be pointing to.

"Do you think we should wake the others up?" she asked.

"You should all sleep for a little longer," I said. "I'll be right back. I have to do something first."

When I stepped outside, there was no sign of Herobrine or Ossie. I found myself walking in the direction Ossie had pointed with her head, my legs itching to run. Going this way led to me to a mine.

I stepped just inside the mine. I could hear the diamonds calling me. Dad said when he made his first diamond sword, the diamonds had called him from the mine. I pulled the iron pickaxe out of my toolkit and got to work.

When I came back a little later, Destiny was asleep and the others were starting to wake up.

"Stevie!" Maison said. "There you are! We woke up and didn't know where you'd gone."

I didn't answer. I'd picked up a stick on my way back from the mine, and I put it and the diamonds on the crafting table. Without a word, Alex, Maison, and Yancy all crowded around me, watching me work. When I was done, I lifted up the diamond sword I had crafted, my own diamond sword.

"Stevie, it's beautiful," Alex said with admiration.

"I had another Herobrine dream," I said. I still felt as if I was in a dream! "What Yancy said is true. Herobrine wants to take over the Overworld and Maison's world. He wants everything. And he said there's another prophecy."

CHAPTER 16

NONE OF US REALLY FELT HUNGRY, BUT WE KNEW we needed food to keep up our energy. I figured I would have to scrounge up something to eat, so I told the others I'd see if there were any fruits or vegetables nearby. Then Yancy said, "Stevie, Stevie, I took care of it. You haven't properly experienced my world until you've eaten one of the staples of our diet: PB and J."

He pulled out a whole bunch of sandwiches he made.

I took a bite and realized that I was hungry. And that it actually tasted pretty good. As we finished eating, Alex picked up the Jack o' Lantern Yancy had grabbed the night before and plunked it right over his head.

"Uh, could you take this off, please?" Yancy asked. "I can barely see a thing."

"Nope," Alex said. "If we pass by people on our travels, we can't have them recognizing you from all the Wanted posters."

"But—" Yancy began.

"None of us are on Wanted posters!" Alex said. "At least not yet, anyway. And I don't want to break you out of any more dungeons."

"Yeah, but if I walk into every tree from here to Herobrine, that will also catch people's attention," Yancy said.

"We'll guide you," Alex said.

Guiding Yancy turned out to be harder than we thought. After we had breakfast and were out walking, following Alex's map, Yancy ran into *a lot* of things. Trees. Rocks. Even a lone sheep. Nothing was safe.

"Can I, um, take this off yet?" Yancy asked after falling over the sheep. "I'm starting to think you guys are pushing me into things on purpose."

"We're not," Alex said. "Just watch where you're going."

"That's what I'm trying to say," Yancy said. "I can't."

It took half a day of walking before we reached the giant forests. By then, Yancy was panting inside his Jack o' Lantern mask and begging, "Please, let me take this off now."

But we were all busy surveying the forest.

"What is it?" Yancy asked. "A hush fell over the crowd, and I don't know why."

"Shh," Alex said. "We're thinking."

The forest was made up of thick, close trees. It circled the mountain, and from where we were standing, we could just see the mountaintop. On it was a teeny, tiny temple. Well, it wasn't really teeny or tiny, but it looked that way from here. If Herobrine was there right now, we were definitely too far away to see.

And there was something else that was weird about the forest. One strip of it heading back to the mountain had trees with zero leaves. But all the other trees we could see in the forest looked untouched. It was almost like that leafless path showed where Herobrine had walked through the area, and all the leaves fell down because of him.

"How should we get through the forest?" I asked.

Alex eyed the darkly-forested areas where the leaves remained. "If we walk under the trees, it's so dark there might be mobs," she mused.

"Something about the leafless path just gives me the creeps," Maison said. "I don't think there will be mobs there because of the light, but . . ." She shuddered. "I guess it feels touched by Herobrine or something. It doesn't feel safe."

"Agreed," Alex said, reaching into her toolkit. "We'll walk over the trees." She tied a lead to one of her arrows and shot the arrow up into the treetops. "Let's climb."

Yancy, Maison, and Destiny all needed some help climbing up that far. Tree climbing wasn't something they learned in schools in their world, which seemed kind of funny, because it was a useful skill to have. Alex and I had to basically haul them up.

When we got on top of the leafed trees, the landscape looked bigger than ever, and dark clouds were starting to ring around the center of the mountain, over the temple.

I clutched my diamond sword. Ever since I was little, I'd dreamed of the day I'd have my own diamond sword, and now that I had one, it didn't feel quite real. I'd always thought when I made my diamond sword, it would be a very festive event and Dad would be proud and it would be a big, growing moment in my life.

Instead, everyone was too scared to be festive, Dad wouldn't care about the sword because he wasn't himself anymore, and instead of feeling like a growing moment, it felt like a desperate attempt to keep Herobrine from taking over the world.

Well, it was a desperate attempt.

As we walked, I thought more about our weapons. Alex had packed a number of weapons in her bag, and I knew Maison was good at fighting. Still, how could I think any of us were even close to being on the same level with Herobrine?

"What is our plan?" I found myself asking as we walked.

"We find Herobrine and take him out," Alex said simply.

"He said he wouldn't be easy to defeat," I murmured, thinking about my dream. "That he'd keep coming back."

"Well, that just means—" Alex began.

She didn't have a chance to finish her thoughts. Something reached out from under the branches and grabbed my foot, pulling me into the darkness below.

CHAPTER 17

I FELL DOWN THROUGH THE LEAVES, LANDING HARD against a branch. The zombie that had grabbed me now hissed in greeting, its dark eyes almost glowing under the shade of the trees.

"Stevie!" I heard the others call from above. I slashed with my diamond sword and took out the zombie in one swipe.

"I—I'm okay," I said shakily. "It was a zombie, but I took care of it."

Zombies climbing up trees like that? I thought. I'd never seen anything like it before. But when Herobrine was around, rules got broken.

Then I blinked. I wasn't alone.

The tree I was on was full of branches, and those branches were covered with zombies, skeletons, and giant spiders. And there was one big sign in front of me that said, WELCOME, STEVIE.

Before the zombies all lunged on me, I managed to shout, "Help!" My diamond sword was stabbing out as fast as possible, but more and more zombies were coming at me, and I heard the screech of spiders right behind them.

Alex came swinging down, cutting through the swarm of zombies and knocking them off me. As the zombies shook themselves and rose again, they all found themselves hit by her arrows. Their hisses stopped as they vanished into nothing.

Maison, Destiny, and Yancy jumped down to the branch next. Yancy had ripped the Jack o' Lantern off his head to see better and shoved it into his backpack. The skeletons on nearby branches also had arrows, and they began shooting at us.

"Take out the zombies and the spiders," Alex said, pulling more arrows from her quiver. "I'll take care of the skeletons."

At once, Maison, Destiny, Yancy, and I hurtled toward the nearby spiders and zombies. A spider reared up before me, red eyes flashing, only to be cut down by my sword. Several zombies veered toward Maison, but she jumped out of their way and turned back on them with her stone sword. Yancy ripped his backpack off his shoulders and swung it around him, knocking zombies off the branch and to the ground far, far below.

The air was full of hisses, screeches and flying arrows. A skeleton's arrow flew toward Yancy, and he blocked it with his backpack, the arrow embedding itself. He pulled the arrow out and began using it as a weapon, keeping the nearby zombies at bay so that Destiny could take them out with her stone sword.

Then everything went into slow motion. First, I saw a skeleton in the next tree over, taking aim at me—at me specifically. And then I saw a creeper sitting there quietly in the middle of all the zombies. The creeper looked at me and started to shake.

No! I thought. The creeper would explode in seconds and we'd all be done for. And I didn't have time to stop the skeleton and stop the creeper at the same time.

"I got it, Stevie!" I heard Alex shouting, her bow drawn back. She leapt, sending the arrow soaring. It hit the skeleton just as the skeleton was releasing its own arrow. The impact of Alex's arrow knocked the skeleton to the side, changing its aim.

"No way," I breathed. The skeleton's arrow shot through the air like a flash of light and hit the creeper, making it disappear in an instant.

"Look!" Maison cried.

When the creeper was hit by the arrow, it had dropped a music disc.

It might be another prophecy! I launched myself across the branch, hitting zombies as I went, and seized the music disc. A spider rose up over me, screeching, and was knocked back by Maison's stone sword. I got up and took out the spider for good with my diamond sword.

I realized then that it had suddenly gone very silent. We'd defeated all the mobs, either with our weapons or by knocking them from the branches.

"Whoa, Alex," Yancy said then, looking at her with big eyes full of appreciation. "That arrow shot—where you got the skeleton and creeper at the same time—that was amazing."

Alex was hurrying over to us, her eyes on the music disc. "I've heard that a music disc can drop from a skeleton shooting a creeper!" she said. "I've just never seen it with my own eyes."

Below, we could hear zombies hissing. Were they climbing back up the trees?

"Quick," I said. "Let's get back on the treetops before any other mobs find us."

When we pulled ourselves up through the leaves and back on the treetops, our visions were flooded with sweet sunlight. The hisses below sounded far away, and I already felt safer.

But when the music disc started to play, I realized we weren't safe at all.

CHAPTER 18

"The only way to defeat Herobrine is together.
Battles there will be, and victory is not for certain.
Together you must work,
but one of you will betray the rest."

"One of us will betray the rest?" I repeated, stammering. I glanced over at everyone, and they looked as shocked as I felt.

Maison would never betray us, I thought, studying her. *She's my best friend.*

Alex would never betray us, I thought. *She's my cousin, and she wants to save the Overworld, too.*

Destiny will never betray us, I thought. *She risked everything to help save the Overworld before.*

Which means . . .

"You!" I said, pulling my sword on Yancy.

"Hey, whoa!" Yancy said, jumping back. "Stevie, take a chill pill!"

I had no idea what that was supposed to mean, and I didn't care. "You're going to betray us!" I said. "You really are working for Herobrine!"

"Hold on," Yancy said. "It says one of us will betray the rest. It doesn't say who!"

"It doesn't take a genius to figure out who it will be!" I said.

"I don't think any of us will betray the rest," Maison said. "Maybe this is just more of Herobrine messing with our heads and trying to turn us against each other."

"Yeah," Alex said. "Yancy saved all of us yesterday. And he just fought with us now. Why would he betray us?"

I stared at them all. How could they not believe me?

"I think Maison and Alex are right," Destiny said. "I think Herobrine just wants to confuse us. Look."

She pointed to the sky. The sun was starting to dip down toward the horizon. It wouldn't be too much longer before dusk. And then . . .

"I think Herobrine wants us to fight so that we waste time and don't show up to the temple until after dark," Destiny said. "He'd want that, because then he'd have a lot more mobs around to help him fight."

My head spun. I didn't want to trust Yancy . . . but I had to admit Maison, Destiny, and Alex all had a good point. Right then, I didn't really feel convinced one way or the other. Still, I knew Destiny was right that we needed to get to the temple before it got dark. And we needed to get off these treetops fast, before any other mobs pulled us under.

Slowly, angrily, I sheathed my sword. "All right," I said. "But I have an idea."

CHAPTER 19

O N TOP OF THE MOUNTAIN STOOD THE RUINED temple. And right in front of the temple stood Herobrine, Ossie in his arms.

Part of me wanted to believe it was another dream, yet this time, I knew it wasn't. There he was, out of my nightmares, out of old ghost stories. He was as real as the rest of us, and I could feel the evil flowing from him and making the air around us hard to breathe. It was as if all the anger and bad feelings in the world came together to form him.

"So you've finally arrived," Herobrine said, staring at us with those blank, wide eyes of his. Without any pupils, his eyes looked like cesspools that could suck you into the depths of them and never let you out.

Herobrine gave a special nod toward Yancy. "My creator," Herobrine said.

"If I'm your creator, I order you to stop this," Yancy said.

Herobrine laughed. "You don't get to order me around. I learned everything I know from you and others like you. I know how to mess with people. I know how to make them feel worthless. I know how to make people who feel worthless turn their anger on other people. I know how to steal what matters most to people." He hugged Ossie extra hard, but without any love. He hugged her like an object he wanted to show belonged to him.

"This stops now, Herobrine," I said. "Give back Ossie!"

"You can't fight me with those puny weapons," Herobrine scoffed. And disappeared.

We all jumped. A moment later, Herobrine reappeared a few feet away, Ossie still in his arms. He smiled at us. "Catch me if you can."

Just like that, he appeared and disappeared like a light blinking on and off. He was there and then he wasn't. The temple shook around us as if we were in an earthquake. The leaves in the forests around us all fell at once.

"Don't you get it?" Herobrine gloated. "This is simply a game to me."

We rushed at him, and as soon as we were close, he was gone again.

Appearing at a new spot, Herobrine went on, "What I've done so far is innocent stuff. I have far more terrible ideas in mind."

Again, we darted toward him. Again, he was gone. We spun around in circles, trying to think of where he would show up next.

"Up here!" Herobrine called. We looked up and he stood on top of the temple.

How do we get up there? I thought. But by then, Herobrine had vanished again.

"Boo," Herobrine said behind my ear. I startled and turned around, only to find nothing behind me. He had left that quickly.

"There's no way to keep him in one spot," Maison whispered to me, clutching her stone sword. The plan I'd come up with wouldn't work unless Herobrine stayed in one spot.

Yancy climbed up one of the columns in the temple. "Hey, Herobrine!" he called. "This is about you and me. Leave everyone else out of it."

Herobrine reappeared near the column, looking up at Yancy. "Oh, but I have so many fun ideas in store!" Herobrine said. "It won't take much more for me to control all of the Overworld. They think I'm an old ghost story here, so they don't take me seriously. And your world will be even easier to take, because most people there haven't even heard of Herobrine. But I'll be in their nightmares soon enough. And then I'll turn those nightmares into a reality."

"Okay," Yancy said. "But you don't know anything about my world."

Herobrine disappeared, then showed back up again, on the other side of the column. He sounded insulted. "People are people," he said. "I know how to turn people against each other. It doesn't matter what world I'm in. And you failed in your attempt to take over the Overworld."

"I know I failed," Yancy said. "But remember, I created you. And think about how much we can accomplish if we work together."

CHAPTER 20

"YANCY, NO!" DESTINY SCREAMED.

"You lied to us!" Alex exclaimed, reaching for her arrows. "You were on his side all along!"

"It's better this way!" Yancy called down to Alex. "Leave your arrows alone. If we work with Herobrine, we won't be destroyed like everyone else. Think about it!"

I'd been right about Yancy this whole time and no one had listened to me! Now we'd led him right to Herobrine, and together they were sure to be unstoppable!

"You traitor!" I roared. If Alex wasn't going to do anything, I was. Blinded by anger, I went running toward the column, drawing my diamond sword.

Herobrine looked at me, amused. Yancy also looked at me, and he winked. Raising my sword, I threw all my weight into hitting Herobrine, making sure to miss Ossie. My sword cracked, and Herobrine continued to stand there, his armor not even dented. In fact, I'd hit him so hard that it reverberated and hurt me, like I'd hit a wall. Herobrine laughed in my face as I crumpled back from the blow.

"Stevie!" Maison cried, and ran to my side.

"I've had a special enjoyment hurting this one," Herobrine said, nodding toward me. "He's weak, but he thinks he's strong. He wants to be his father, no matter what he says. He wants to be known as the most feared mob slayer around. Well, little boy, I stood still and let you get a good shot at me. What happened?"

Maison was helping me get up, but I was still wincing in pain and I couldn't stand without her help. The next thing I knew, Alex and Destiny were beside me. In Herobrine's arms, Ossie was scratching and trying to get loose, though her claws didn't even faze Herobrine.

"Yeah, it's funny how people who act like they're strong are usually pretty weak," Yancy said. "What shall we call the world we make together? Yancytopia? Herobrineland?"

"We won't be making any world together," Herobrine replied. "You can help me, my creator, but I call the shots now. Nevertheless, if you really please me, I'm willing to make you second-in-command."

"No, Yancy!" Destiny said. "Don't do it! You're better than this! I know you are!"

"I don't know," Yancy said, stroking his chin with his fingers as if considering this. "Second-in-command sounds better than just being defeated. And who are we to think we can defeat Herobrine? I mean, come on! It's Herobrine! We might as well bow down to him as King Herobrine now!"

"King Herobrine of Herobrineland," Herobrine mused to himself. "I like the sound of that. I just need a crown."

"I have the perfect one for you," Yancy said, reaching into his backpack.

Herobrine smiled hungrily. "Yes, crown me," he said.

Yancy pulled the Jack o' Lantern out of his backpack and threw it down over Herobrine's head. Herobrine, not expecting this, jolted and tried to rip the Jack o' Lantern off his head. In the process, he dropped Ossie, who skittered away to safety. "Agh!" he yelled. "I can't see!"

"Now!" Yancy yelled to us. "Get him!"

CHAPTER 21

E WERE ON HIM IMMEDIATELY. ALEX YANKED out multiple arrows, lined her bow, and sent them flying. Maison and Destiny dove at Herobrine with their swords. Even Ossie leapt back at Herobrine, digging her claws into her kidnapper and hissing violently.

I hadn't regained all my strength, but there wasn't time. With all the force I still had left in me, I threw myself at Herobrine, hitting him with my diamond sword. This time the sword glowed a bright, lightning blue, sending sparks through the temple when it hit him. Cracked sword or no, I saw Herobrine's armor split from the impact.

Yancy jumped down from the column. "Nice try, Herobrine!" he shouted, flinging out at Herobrine with his backpack. "But I'm not like that anymore!"

Then it happened. We all hit him at the same time. Arrows, swords, even that silly backpack. A bright burst of light shot out of my sword, exploding up toward the sky. Herobrine screamed in rage and disappeared.

The clouds went away from the sky. The forests around us immediately grew back all their leaves. And the evil feeling went away, letting us all breathe in fresh, clear air again.

Ossie jumped up into my arms, purring. I hugged her, relieved that she was in my arms again.

"Fan out!" Alex called. "See if he's still in the temple."

"No, he's not," Yancy said. I saw his hands were shaking. "His presence isn't here. He's gone."

Alex marched right up to Yancy, glaring him in the eye. He shrank back a little.

"You!" Alex said, pointing at him with one of her arrows. "Don't ever scare me like that again!"

Yancy sighed with relief that this was all she was upset about. "I didn't mean to scare you!" he said. "But I created Herobrine, and I kind of know how he thinks. I knew flattery would distract him. Otherwise, he was going to keep appearing and disappearing like he was doing. And I thought about the prophecy and I figured it'd be a good way to fake him."

"Yeah, well, for a moment there, I thought you were serious," Alex said.

"I did, too," Destiny admitted.

"I winked at Stevie to try to let him know I was faking it," Yancy said. "It's not like I could tell you guys anything with Herobrine right there."

"That's why you winked?" I said. "I thought . . . I thought it was just you mocking me."

"Mocking you?" Yancy said. "Stevie, we're a team now. Friends?"

He held out his hand, smiling. Still a little uneasy, I took his hand and shook it.

"Friends," I said, awkwardly.

We searched around the temple and the mountain-top. No sign of Herobrine.

"Your idea worked!" Maison said to me.

"Yeah," I said, hugging Ossie close. When the prophecies were talking about how we had to all work together, I wondered if that meant we had to all attack Herobrine at the same time because otherwise we wouldn't be strong enough. We needed real teamwork.

"You created him," Destiny said, looking to Yancy. "Do you really think he's gone?"

"He's gone from here," Yancy said. "But is he *gone* gone? I don't think so. I think we weakened him. The Overworld should be safe right now, though I don't know how long until he returns."

I thought back on the prophecies, too. They had promised that Herobrine wouldn't be easy to beat and he'd be back. Did that mean that one of us was still going to betray the others? Or did that prophecy just predict how Yancy was going to *pretend* to betray us so we'd be able to get Herobrine?

We looked out on the horizon as the sun drifted farther down. From here, the Overworld looked so vast, yet it also looked so fragile.

"If Herobrine is still out there, we're ready for him," Alex said, adjusting the quiver on her shoulder. "Now that we've seen him, we have a better idea of who he is and how to fight him. This will give us more time to plan. We can also search for more prophecies."

Ossie purred and licked my face. Holding her, I looked down at the diamond sword I'd made. It had a little crack in it, but I could fix that. This sword had just helped save the whole Overworld.

"So, what should we do tonight?" Destiny asked.

After studying my sword, I sheathed it. "Let's make camp here tonight," I said. "It will be dark before we can get anywhere."

"We'll take turns with who guards," Alex said. "I'll start, then it can be Stevie, Maison, Destiny, and Yancy."

"Aww," Yancy said. "You trust me now."

"In the morning, we'll head back to Stevie's home and make more plans," Maison said. "I think we're all going to sleep well tonight. And hopefully, we'll all have nice dreams!"

"Yes," I said. "And whatever it takes, we're going to keep the Overworld safe."

To be continued . . . .